This book is dedicated to my Grandson

JEFFERY

Since the day you were born, I knew you could do anything!
Believe in yourself and practice, practice, practice!

I Love You

Granny

Love,
Nanette
2018

Blue
The Frog

Written by Nanette

Illustrations by Pat Thompson

Edited By Ruth H. and Stephanie Taylor

Library of Congress Control Number 2003093991
ISBN 0-9741269-2-6

Published by St. Bernard Publishing
P.O. Box 2218 ♥ Bay City MI 48707-2218 ♥ 989-892-1348

Little Red, the cow and Granny were walking to their special tree on Granny's Farm. It stood tall and was mighty strong. Three of its huge branches formed a private, cozy little seat. They often sat there to talk and to spend time together.

"Granny! Granny! What is that **Blue** thing under the tree?" asked Little Red.

"I don't know, Little Red! Let's go take a look," said Granny.

Resting in a clump of grass was a frog - a **Blue** frog! It seemed as though something was wrong. Very wrong! Granny picked him up and saw that he only had three legs - two in the front and one in the back.

"Oh, dear!" said Granny. "He's very weak. Let's take the **Blue** frog to the barn and take care for him."

"Granny, do you think he's going to be all right? Do you think we can call him **Blue**? Can he stay here? Can he, please?" asked Little Red.

"Yes, Little Red, he will be just fine. Settle down and don't worry. I think **Blue** will be a good name for him. He may stay and live with us if that is what he wants to do," answered Granny.

Granny and Little Red took care of **Blue** night and day. They gave him food, water and a lot of love. A couple of days later, **Blue** felt a little better and Granny carried him outside to get some fresh air.

Blue sat in the soft green grass and noticed a bunch of bugs. He had never seen so many different bugs and all of them were moving. He saw some crawling, walking and jumping! Blue was fascinated and sat completely still. His bulging eyes watched and watched the bugs for a long time. Soon he started to move his front legs and slowly drag his back leg.

"Granny! Granny!" yelled Little Red. "Come and see what Blue is doing!"

Granny turned and watched **Blue's** clumsy movements. She saw how difficult it was for him to shift his body.

"**Blue**, are you ever going to be able to jump?" asked Little Red.

"JUMP? I didn't know I was supposed to jump!" croaked **Blue**.

Granny heard their conversation and decided to speak to them. First, Granny took Little Red to their special tree. They sat on the cozy little seat while Granny explained **Blue's** problem to her.

10

"Little Red," said Granny, "if **Blue** does some exercises to strengthen his legs and back, he may be able to jump some day."

"Really!" said Little Red

"Really and even if he can't we will still love him," answered Granny.

Then, Granny took **Blue** to the special tree. She said, "**Blue**, if you want to learn how to jump, you need to do some exercises and after that - it's practice, practice, practice! Do you want me to show you now?"

"Oh yes!" shouted Blue.

Granny squatted down and leaned forward. She placed her hands on the ground and started to do the exercises.

"Granny, I can't do that. I don't have two back legs, remember?" said Blue.

"Oh yes, you can! All you have to do is practice, remember! Your legs will get stronger every day. I know you can do this and so does Little Red," said Granny.

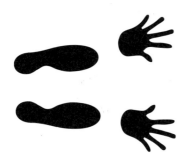

Blue was glad to hear that they believed in him. He tried and tried to jump. Sometimes he fell over sideways and other times he would land right on his head. He used his one back leg to push off and his front legs for balancing and land-ing, but nothing seemed to be working.

Each day **Blue** would practice and practice and practice. And guess what happened? **Blue** finally did it. He could JUMP! He could JUMP! He was so excited, but he didn't want anyone to know just yet. He wanted to practice a little bit more before he showed Granny and Little Red how well he could jump. Then, after a few more days, he was ready.

"Granny! Granny! Little Red! Little Red! Where is everyone?" shouted **Blue**.

No one answered.

"Granny! Little Red!" **Blue** yelled again as they came out of the barn. "I have something to show you."

Blue quickly JUMPED from one spot to another - just like all the other frogs. It was a little crooked, but he didn't fall sideways or land on his head. He was actually jumping! They all clapped their hands and shouted with glee. Granny was right! **Blue** now believed he could do anything if he practiced and practiced and practiced.

After they settled down from all the excitement, Granny said, "We have a small problem and we'll have to work on it together. Now that **Blue** can jump, he should also be able to swim. We need to clean up the pond and make it safe for him."

Granny, Little Red and **Blue** worked for hours moving the rocks, dead leaves and branches from the pond. They planted flowers, lily pads, cattails and long grasses for shade and food.

After the work was done, Granny and Little Red were exhausted and fell asleep right next to the flowers. **Blue** leaped into the pond, sat on a lily pad and enjoyed the warm afternoon sun.

All of a sudden, **Blue** spotted something and shouted, "Granny! Granny! Wake up! There is something **BLACK** in the water. What is that? Is it an animal? It's moving!"

Visit Granny and all her friends on her website!
www.lifeongrannysfarm.com